ELOISE

TAKES ~A~ BAWTH

for Marian
–J. H. & J. S.

for D.D.
who brought me
to Kay
–H. K.

SIMON & SCHUSTER BOOKS FOR YOUNG READERS An imprint of Simon & Schuster Children's Publishing Division • 1230 Avenue of the Americas, New York, New York 10020 • Text copyright © 2002 by the Estate of Kay Thompson • Illustrations by Hilary Knight copyright © 2002 by the Estate of Kay Thompson • All rights reserved • SIMON & SCHUSTER BOOKS FOR YOUNG READERS is a trademark of Simon & Schuster. • Book design by Hilary Knight & Dan Potash • Printed in USA • First Edition • LC: 2002004115 • ISBN 0-689-84288-0 • 10 9 8 7 6 5 4 3 2 1

KAY THOMPSON'S
ELOISE
TAKES A BAWTH

drawings by
HILARY KNIGHT

additional plumbing by
MART CROWLEY

SIMON & SCHUSTER BOOKS FOR YOUNG READERS
NEW YORK   LONDON   TORONTO   SYDNEY   SINGAPORE

"ELOISE"

Nanny says
"please don't dawdle
I want you in that tub
and out of that tub
on the dub dub double

We must be
clean as clean can be

Mr. Salomone
the sweetest old manager
in this sweet old world
busy busy busy
with the Venetian Masked Ball
in the Grawnd Ballroom
tonight
is being polite
by taking a break
and coming to tea"

Nanny is full of spit and polish

And I say
"In that case Nanny dear
my mostly companion
I'll have to wash Weenie
and soak Skipperdee"

"Well
ELOISE
Now is not the time for
a slap-dash puddle
I want all of you ready
dressed neat and nicely
hair shampooed and brushed
precisely in hawlf an hour"

You have to be absolutely careful
when you take a bawth in a hotel

The absolutely first thing you have to do
is close that door and lock it
and push that scale across that crack
to be certain in case
somebody looks in behind your back
or walks in
in front of your face
like Room Service

Then you have to glawnce
out the window
and say hello
to the pigeons
specially
when
you
are
in

THE
most
terriblest
rush
but
won't won't won't
let on
and
pretend
you
have
all
the
time
in this sweet old world
which of course you absolutely don't
for Lord's sake

Next you have to
turn on all of these taps

and fling on
all of these faucets

and handle all of these handles

and let that water gush out and slush out
into that sweet old tub tub tub
and fill it up to the absolutely
top of its brim so that it can
slip over its rim onto the floor
                    if it wants to

I like to have a tub
that's rawther full

You skibble into the bawthroom
and take off all of your clothes

PLOOP

and
look in
the mirror
awhile
in
some
adorable
pose

Then
you open your
dear little
mouth

and raise
your dear
little voice

and sing your dear little heart out

Oh I absolutely love
taking a bawth

Oh there is nothing so refreshing as a bawth

You skibble into the bathroom
and take off all your clothes

and look in the mirror awhile
in some adorable pose

And you're absolutely nude
from up your nose down to your toes

Oh I absolutely love
It's pure heaven from above

Oh I absolutely love
taking a bawth

"Mr. Salomone what's going on?
The food is flooded
The wine is watery, the servers are slipping
I'm afraid the seafood may swim off the plates
This ball will be a flop
if it doesn't stop
before the guests arrive"

It's pure heaven from above

Nanny says
"Eloise
hush hush hush
Someone is calling on the telephone

Halloooooo?
Mr. Salomone?
What's that you say?

You might be late
for our tea tea tea?"

"Nanny there seems to be a glitch
in the plans for the Venetian Masked Ball
A drip has begun to drop within
the walls of the stately old Plaza
I've got to find out what's up"

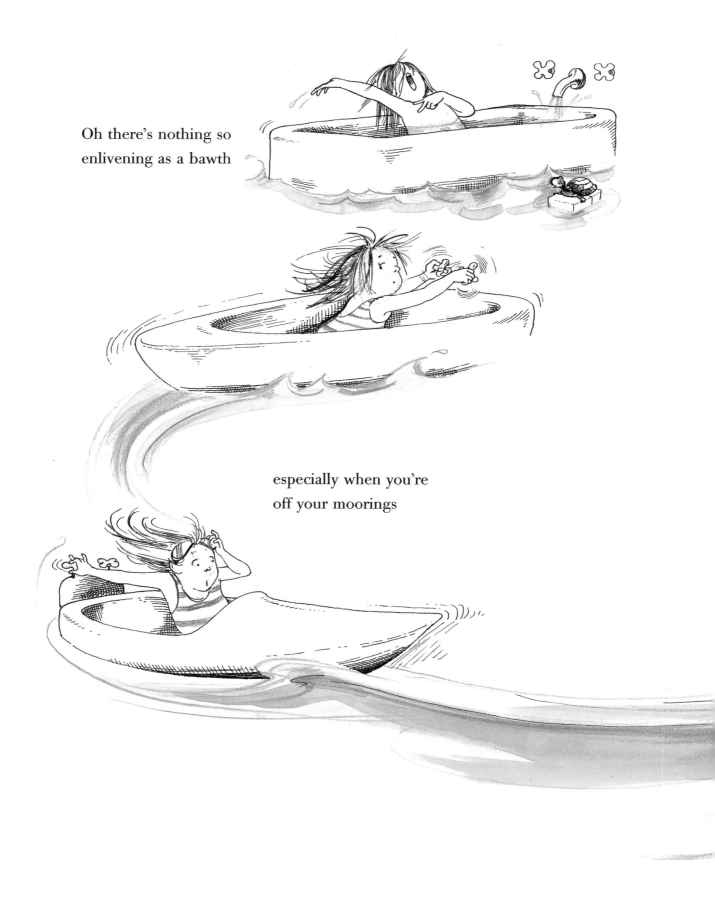

Oh there's nothing so
enlivening as a bawth

especially when you're
off your moorings

and you have to go full throttle

I better get this going at a
comfortable speed of about
six hundred miles an hour
So hang on
barupp barupp barupp

Being dry is not allowed

There is nothing
so refreshing

WELCOME
STAR!

SPLAWSH

Sometimes I'm just
the loosest cannonball
in all the Caribbean

MAYDAY MAYDAY MAYDAY
This battle's absolutely lost
so lash yourselves to the mast
and hang on to your mustache kids
this water's sinking fast
BABOOM
BABOOM
BLAST BLAST BLAST
Advise all these ships at sea
WARNING
WARNING
Cape Hatteras to Cape Cod and Cape Town too
batten all your hatches down with glue glue glue
and as for all you itsy bitsy small craft
treat yourself to a lifesaver or better yet a life raft
SOS
SOS
AVOW AND AVAST

It's cannon fire as thick as steam
We're done for in this wind and rain
We're either going down with the ship
or else we're going down the drain
SEND UP ALL YOUR SIGNAL FLARES
RAH RAH RAH
Now hear this all you foghorns
Blow your stacks off quick
We've gotta get out of this tub tub tub
before we're absolutely SEESAW SICK

And sometimes
I'm Little Miss Mermaid
but let's keep that
between us

Oh what a festival
these
fish
fish
fish
and chips

Ah those scrumptious shrimp
gurgle
gurgle
gurgle

and chewy water chestnuts

but oh my Lord
this seaweed
is sawlty

Here's what I like to do
dive for the odd coin

Oh there's nothing so inviting

"ELOISE dear
Mr. Salomone's
on the line
and says
the Head Engineer's lips
are looking
white white white"

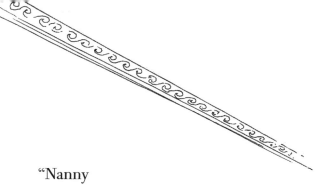

"Nanny
the place is awash
There are drips in the walls
There are puddles in the halls
The masked ball
is sunk
We must find the leak"

WE INTERRUPT YOUR VERY FAVORITE SOAP OPERA
TO BRING YOU
LIVE FROM THE PLAZA HOTEL

THE LATEST BREAKING NEWS

TONIGHT
HERE IN THE MIDDLE
OF MIDTOWN MANHATTAN
THE FAMOUS PLAZA HOTEL

SPRANG A LEAK

JUST AS THE CHARITY PARTY
THE VENETIAN MASKED BALL
WAS GETTING UNDER WAY
IN THE GRAND BALLROOM!

We'll swim the English Channel
to Scotland and to Wales
We couldn't swim any fawster if we were fish
and we had fins and tails

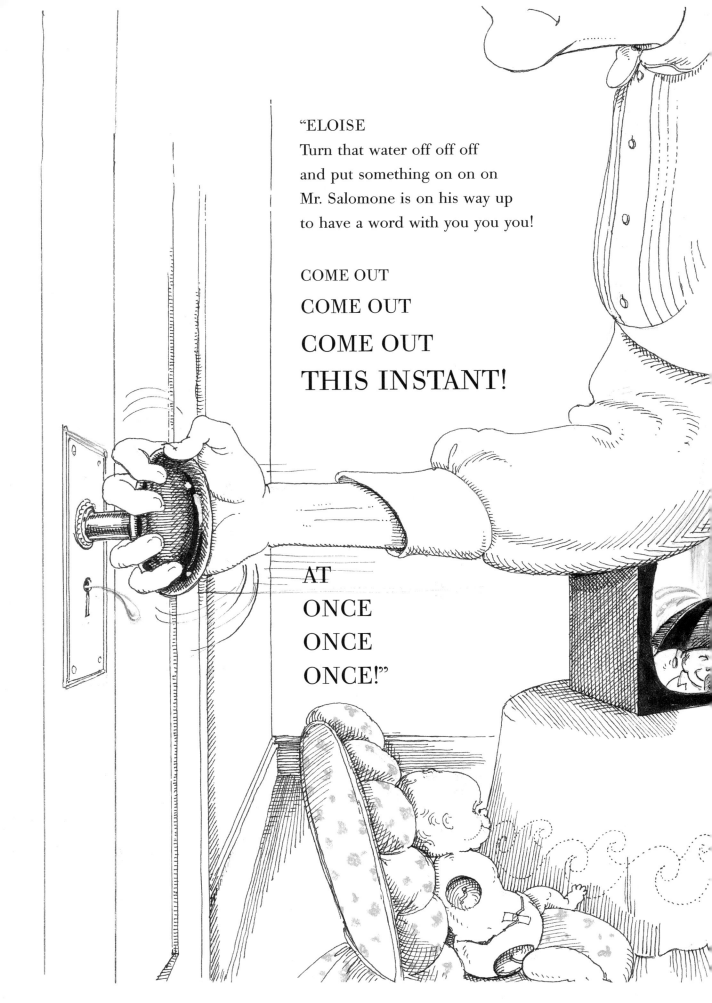

"ELOISE
Turn that water off off off
and put something on on on
Mr. Salomone is on his way up
to have a word with you you you!

COME OUT

COME OUT

COME OUT

THIS INSTANT!

AT
ONCE
ONCE
ONCE!"

SPLAWSH

on the glub
glub glubble

"ELOISE
Mr. Salomone
wants to talk to you
His hotel is a wreck wreck wreck"

"Oh Nanny dear
it's not my fault
After all I'm only six
and have been at sea
for three weeks"

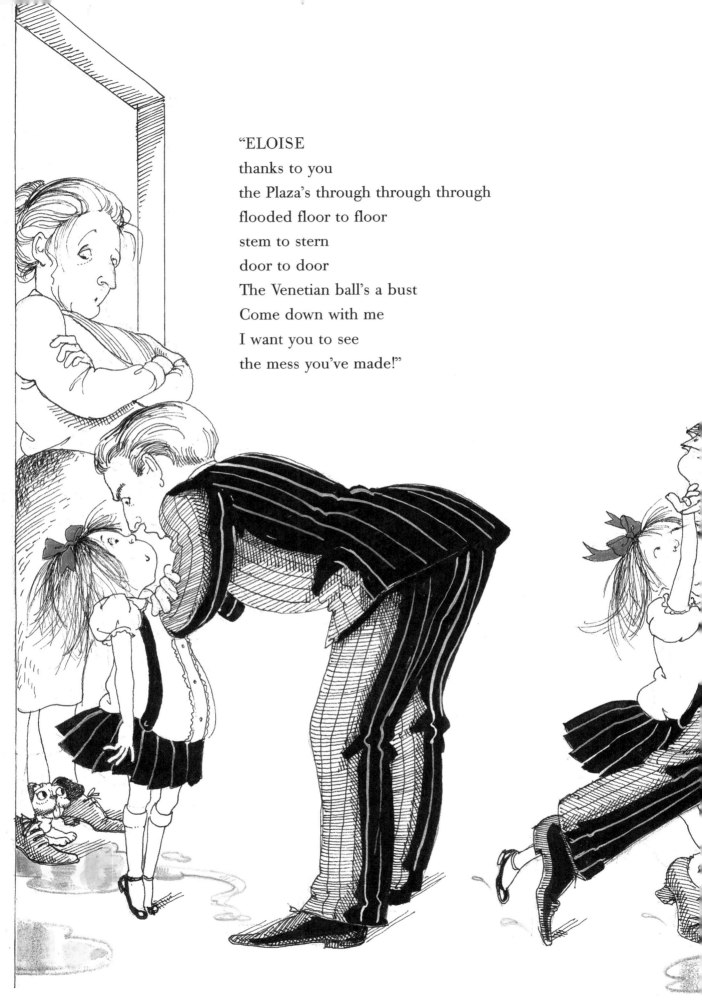

"ELOISE
thanks to you
the Plaza's through through through
flooded floor to floor
stem to stern
door to door
The Venetian ball's a bust
Come down with me
I want you to see
the mess you've made!"

TO WHOEVER FINDS THIS

Some say "Eloise Takes a Bawth" was lost at sea for forty years. Others swear it was locked up in a credenza in Venice and dried out only recently. Only Eloise knows the real story, and she's not talking.

There is some evidence, though, that "Eloise Takes a Bawth" was born in the brain of Kay Thompson as she soaked in a hot tub in Rome after writing "Eloise in Moscow." She summoned Hilary Knight to the Eternal City and there they worked on the "Bawth" for four years. Their mutual pal, playwright Mart Crowley, stepped in from time to time, adding sage counsel, élan, and the occasional drop of wisdom. Even though "Eloise Takes a Bawth" was cataloged by Harper & Row in 1964, the book was never published (artistic differences, for Lord's sake).

In 2001, Miss Thompson's heirs decreed that "Eloise Takes a Bawth" should be brought to an eager public. Mr. Knight set to work creating art from sketches he'd drawn forty years ago. Mr. Crowley pieced together the many drafts of Miss Thompson's text. And Miss Thompson's niece and nephew supervised the whole, along with my colleagues at Simon & Schuster.

Now Eloise's forty-year bawth is finally drawn. Soak away.

                                    -The Editor